I DO NOT LIKE AL'S HAT

Erin McGill

Greenwillow Books
An Imprint of HarperCollins*Publishers*

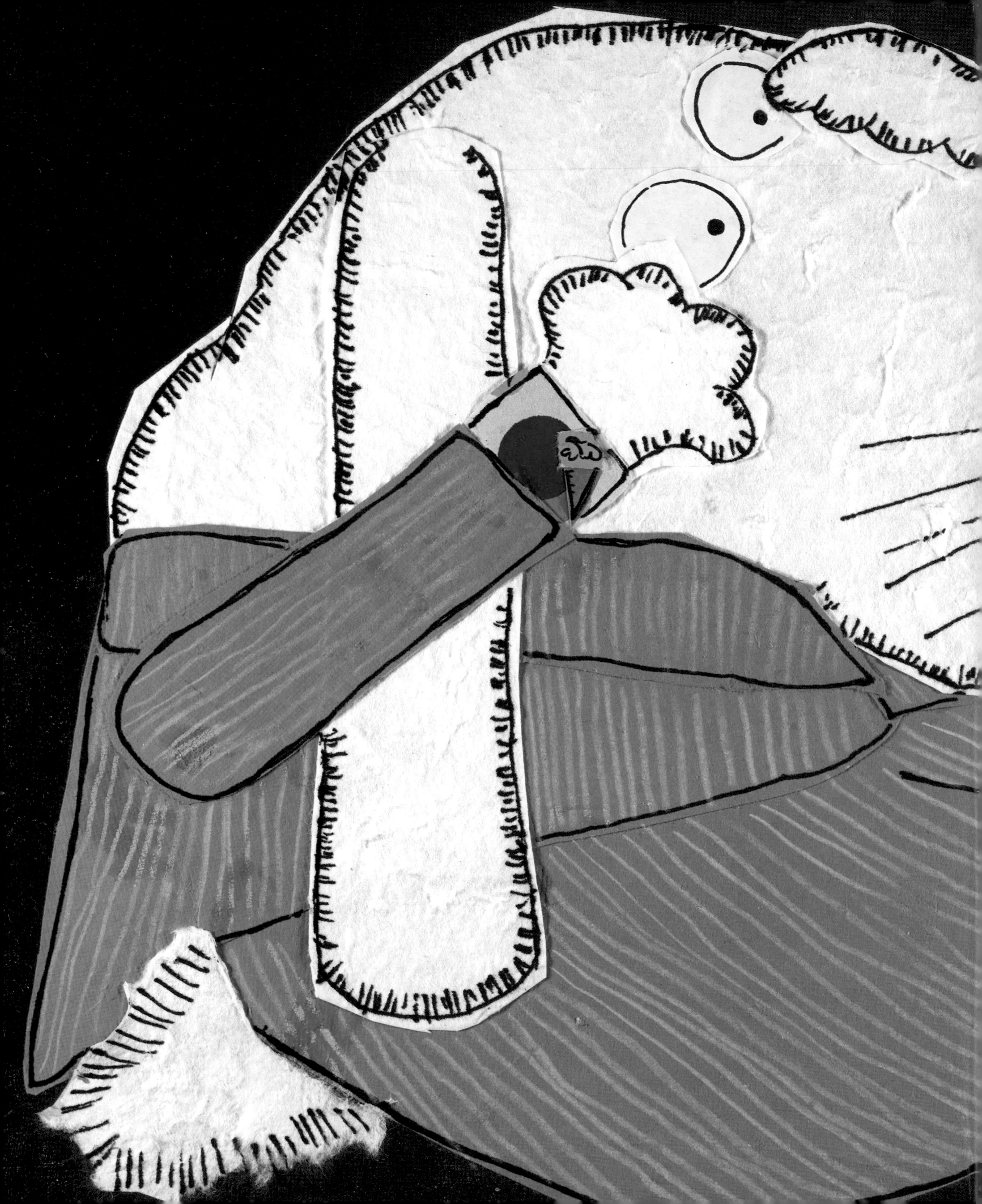

Another night in Abracadabra Al's hat.

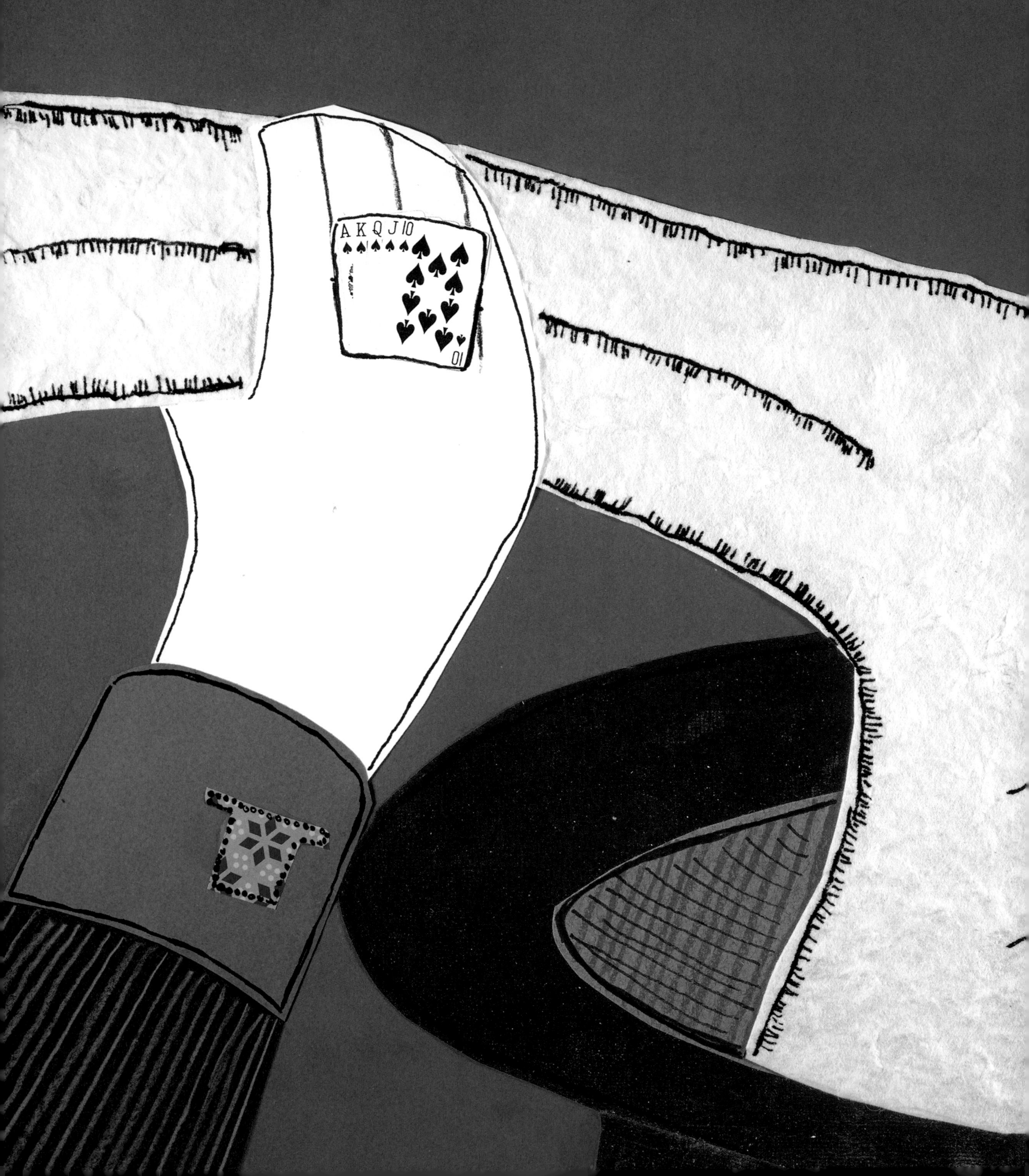
A K Q J 10

What is a magic show without a rabbit coming out of a hat?

I do not like Al's hat.

I do like the spotlight.
I do like the applause.
And I do like the carrots.

CLAP! CLAP! CLAP! CLAP! CLAP!

CLAP!
CLAP!
CLAP!
CLAP!

But that is not enough. My ears have had enough.

I need a new job.

What else can I do?

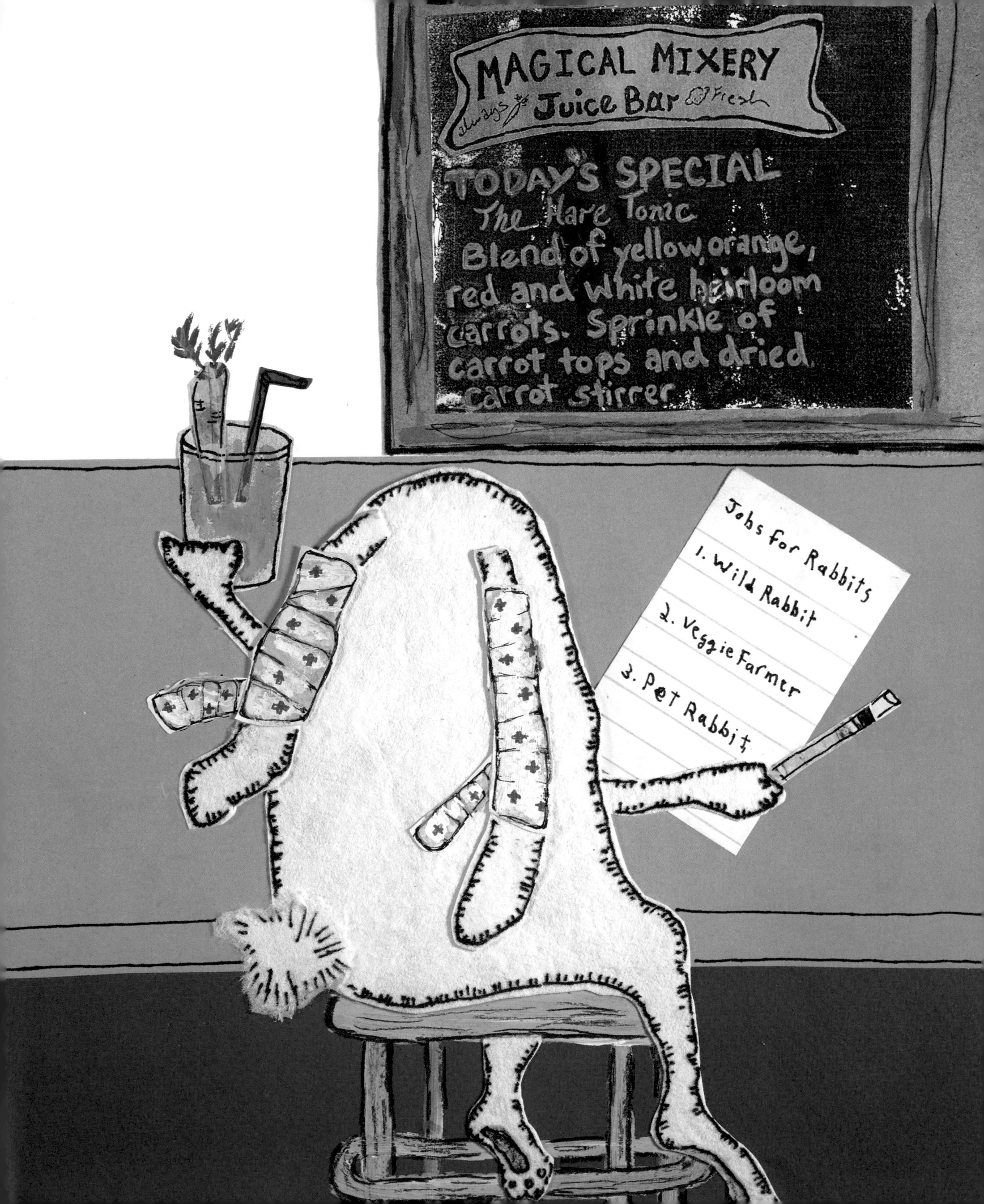
MAGICAL MIXERY
always Juice Bar Fresh
TODAY'S SPECIAL
The Hare Tonic
Blend of yellow, orange, red and white heirloom carrots. Sprinkle of carrot tops and dried carrot stirrer
Jobs for Rabbits
1. Wild Rabbit
2. Veggie Farmer
3. Pet Rabbit

Being a wild rabbit could be exciting . . .
my ears blowing in the breeze,
the open road, adventures.

FREEWAY
Route
10

But I do not think I am cut out

for the wild life.

Being a farmer seems much less dangerous—
my very own farm, the great outdoors,
all the vegetables I can eat.

Herb's Hundred-Acre Farm

I do not think I am cut out

for farming, either.

Pet rabbit it is!

This job looks right to me.

Carrot Chronicle
Classifieds
Dentist
Keep your Chompers Chomping
AT DR. DAN'S
Pet Rabbits Wanted
Sophie 4 years old
145 Lake Drive
Nice house with lots of grass and vegetable garden.
Looking for a very fluffy rabbit to be best friends. Likes to play dress-up and put on shows. Please come right away if you are the right rabbit.
There will be cake!
Custom Clothes
For the handsome hare
Tommy 5 years old
22 Main Street
Looking for a rabbit who likes to play video games and baseball. Must be able to play catch and swing a bat.

"Hello, I'm Herb.
I saw your ad for a pet rabbit.
I am here for the position."

"Hi, I'm Sophie.
Hop in, Herb.
Let's go for a ride!"

“You are just in time for the show,” said Sophie.

"We can be anything
we want to be,"
said Sophie.

CLAP!

CLAP!

CLAP!

"Hooray!
Now let's have cake!"

"Herb, will you stay
and be my best friend?" asked Sophie.

And spend another day with Sophie? **YES!**
Because I do like the spotlight,
I do like the applause,
and I do like carrot . . . cake.

But I love Sophie most of all!

In memory of my mother

www.harpercollinschildrens.com

Cut paper, ink, and gouache were used to prepare the full-color art.
The text type is 24-point Cardigan Bold.

Library of Congress Cataloging-in-Publication Data is available.
ISBN 978-0-06-245576-5 (trade ed.)
"Greenwillow Books."

17 18 19 20 SCP 10 9 8 7 6 5 4 3 2 1
First Edition

Greenwillow Books